For Elliot xx ~ J. P.

tiger tales

5 River Road, Suite 128, Wilton, CT 06897

Published in the United States 2019

Originally published in Great Britain 2019

by Little Tiger Press Ltd.

Text and illustrations by Joanne Partis

Text and illustrations copyright © 2019 Little Tiger Press Ltd.

ISBN-13: 978-1-68010-174-4

ISBN-10: 1-68010-174-9

Printed in China

LTP/1400/2647/0219

For more insight and activities, visit us at www.tigertalesbooks.com

Oh, NO, BEAR!

BY JOANNE PARTIS

tiger tales

Hello, Bear!
Bear has woken up
and he is HUNGRY!

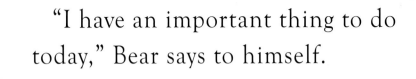

"I have an important thing to do today," Bear says to himself.

"Now, what is it . . . ?"

Bear's list of things to do today.
1. Eat
2. Sleep

A wonderful smell is wafting through the forest.
It is **very** distracting!

Sniff . . .

Sniff . . .

Bear has an amazing nose. It is very good at following delicious smells.

And delicious smells like this can mean only one thing. FOOD!

"Hello, Bear!" It's Rabbit and her friends.
They're very busy digging up carrots.

What an **enormous** pile!
"Try a carrot!" offers Rabbit.
"Well, if you insist," says Bear.

"This one is good," Bear says to himself, with a nibble. "And this one is particularly . . .

. . . CARROTY.

And I'll just have a little taste of this one . . . ."

OH, NO, BEAR!

Oh, dear.
The wheelbarrow of carrots
seems to be empty.

"Where are our carrots?"
asks Rabbit. "We spent all
day picking them!"

"I'm sorry," mumbles Bear. "I only meant to
have a few."
Bear looks at the field of carrots waiting
to be picked. But before he can think of a
very helpful idea, his nose begins to tingle.

Another wonderful smell is wafting past.

Bear forgets all about helping poor Rabbit
and sets off after it.

Be careful where you're stepping, Bear!

"Hello, Bear!" says Squirrel. She's been very busy picking tasty acorns with her friends.

To a bear with a hungry tummy and an amazing nose, acorns smell fantastic!

"Would you like to help us pick some?" asks Squirrel. "You can try some, too!"

"Yes, please!" says Bear eagerly. "Mmmm," he munches happily. It is hard to say much with a large mouthful of tasty acorns.

"Mmmmm,

MMMmm,

MMMMM!"

OH, NO, BEAR!

Oh, dear. It happened again.

"You were supposed to fill up the baskets, not your tummy!" grumbles Squirrel.

It is incredible how many acorns will fit in a hungry bear's tummy.

"I'm sorry," says Bear. "Maybe I could help you find some more acorn trees." Bear looks around but . . .

Sniff . . .

It's very hard to concentrate when . . .

sniff . . .

another tempting smell comes drifting through the trees.

"SLOW DOWN, BEAR!"

"Hello, Bear," waves Beaver. "Look at the big fish I've caught for my dinner."

"I won't eat Beaver's fish," Bear says to himself.
He is sure that he can resist eating the food this time.

"Have a little taste if you like!" shouts Beaver.

Oh, dear.
Bear has accidentally eaten
Beaver's fish.

"That was supposed to be
my dinner!" moans Beaver.

"I was trying so hard not to
eat it," says Bear sadly. "I
wonder if there are more fish
in the river."

Bear jumps in . . . .

SPLASH!

"No," he sputters. "None in here."

Bear can't find any fish at all. Where have they gone?

"I'm sorry, Beaver," says Bear gloomily. "I ate the only fish in the whole river."

Time to get going, Bear thinks.

Poor Bear. Things really haven't gone right today at all.

"I shouldn't have eaten Beaver's fish," says Bear to himself, rubbing his rather large belly.

"Or Squirrel's acorns.

OR Rabbit's carrots."

What if Bear's friends are angry with him? And what if they go hungry all winter?

"I will go right back to my cave to do some extra hard thinking," yawns Bear, suddenly feeling v e r y s l e e p y.

"I will think of a way to make all my friends happy again."

But when he gets home, Bear can't squeeze
through the front door.
Bear is very confused.

He's **sure** he lived here this morning!

Poor Bear.

He is wet and tired and full, and now his house is
the wrong size, too!

He squeezes and wriggles, but it's no good. He just
won't fit.

"I'm stuck!" he cries.

He really is a sad bear.

But who's this coming through the forest?

"Hello, Bear!" call his friends. "We've come to thank you."

"You dug up all these carrots," says Rabbit.

"And bumped the trees to make the acorns fall," says Squirrel.

"And you caught all the fish in the river!" says Beaver.

Bear waves his legs in reply. He feels a little silly as his friends have to talk to his bottom.

"Now let us help you!" says Rabbit kindly.

They **heave** and they **push** until . . .

P O P!

Bear is in! It is the right house after all!
"Thank you, everyone," smiles Bear sleepily.
"Did I really help all of you even though I ate
your food?"

"You really did," says Beaver.
"And you always eat a lot when it's
time to hibernate!" adds Squirrel.
"Hibernate!" yawns Bear happily.
"That's the important thing I have
to remember . . . to . . . do."

Good night, Bear.
See you in the spring!

Bear's list of
things to
do today.
1. Eat
2. Sleep